DIG A TUNNEL

by Ryan Ann Hunter
illustrated by Edward Miller

Holiday House / New York

For Jack and Jane, who keep me wondering —E. G. M.

Thanks, Candy, Greg, and Melanie, for great childhood memories —P. D. G.

For my parents —E. M.

The authors would like to thank Walter C. Grantz,
Chief Engineer of the Chesapeake Bay Bridge and
Tunnel District, for his assistance.

Digging tunnels can be extremely dangerous,
because they sometimes collapse. Never try
to dig your own tunnel.

Library of Congress Cataloging-in-Publication Data
Hunter, Ryan Ann.
    Dig a Tunnel / by Ryan Ann Hunter ; illustrated by Edward Miller III
— 1st ed.
        p.   cm.
    Summary: Simply describes a variety of tunnels, how they are built
and how they are used.
    ISBN 0-8234-1391-8
    1. Tunneling—Juvenile literature. 2. Tunnels—Juvenile literature.
[1. Tunnels.] I. Miller, Ed, 1964–   ill. II. Title.
TA807.H86   1999
624.1' 93—dc21   98-5380   CIP   AC

Moles dig tunnels.
So do prairie dogs.

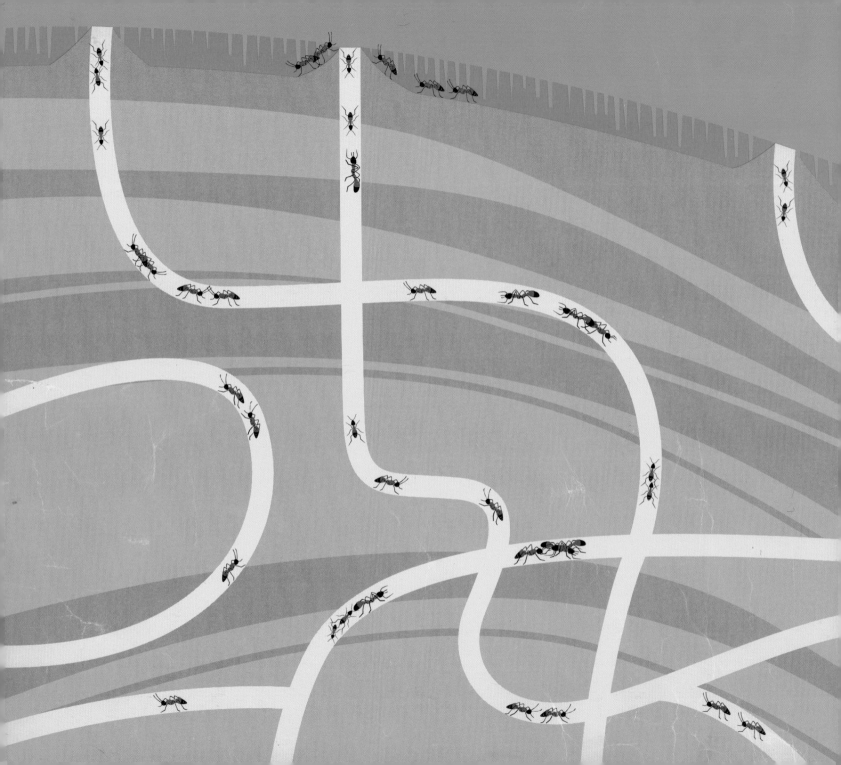

Ants hook miles of tunnels together in a maze.
But they never get lost.
When people saw how animals tunneled through the
ground, they must have thought, *What a great idea!*

The first long tunnels people dug were used for water.

Then warriors dug tunnels under castle walls to sneak inside.

Prisoners dug tunnels to escape.

Bank robbers dug tunnels, too.

Miners still use tunnels to go deep into the earth to find gold and silver and other treasures.

In South Africa, the diamond mining tunnels are so deep the rock walls are hot!

Now we use tunnels more than ever before. People and all kinds of things people need travel through tunnels in cars and trucks and buses and trains.

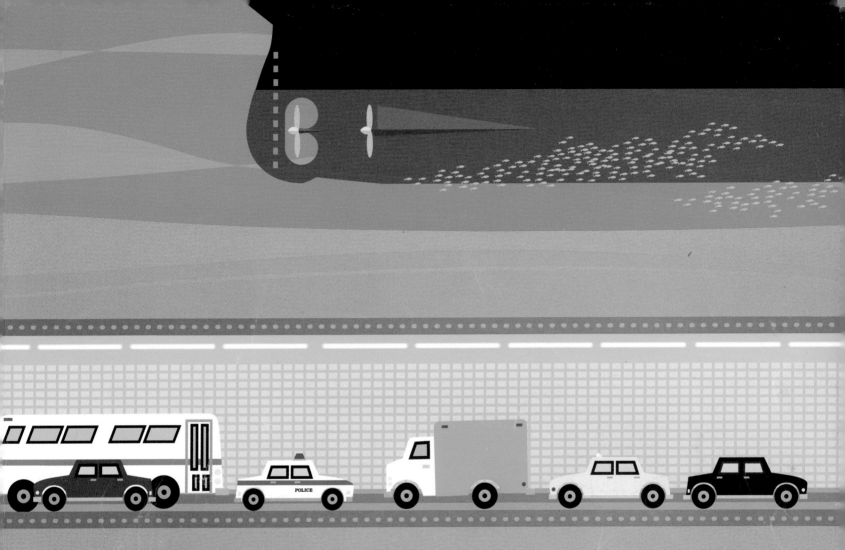

Tunnels go under rivers and bays.
The **Chesapeake Bay Bridge-Tunnel** has more than 3,000 lights on the tunnel walls to keep the roadway bright while you drive through.

ENGLAND

The **Chunnel** takes you under the
English Channel in 19 minutes.

FRANCE

Some tunnels go right through mountains.
The **Mont Blanc Car Tunnel** cuts 7
miles straight through the Alps.
In France, they'll wave good–bye
to you. *Au revoir!*

FRANCE

In Italy, they'll wave hello. *Buon giorno!*

ITALY

Long ago people had to use fire, hammers, and chisels to dig a tunnel.

Now we use dynamite and big machines. One is nicknamed the mole!

5

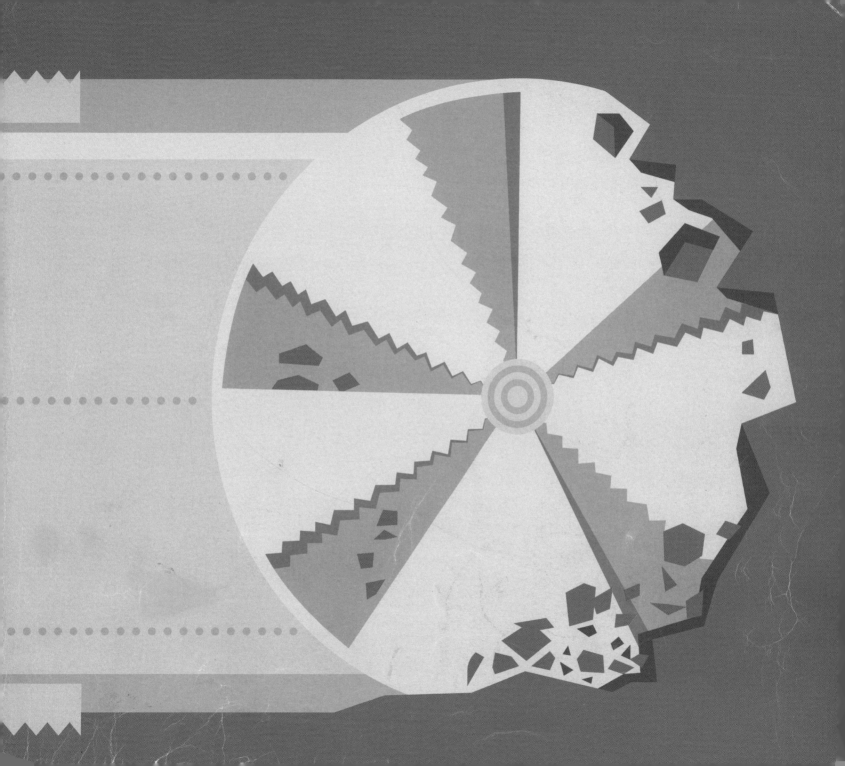

Tunnels are made in different ways.
You can start at each end and meet in the middle.
Or you can go all the way from one side to the other.
Laser beams help keep the tunnel straight.

It's not easy.

You need to haul the dirt away. And have fresh air to breathe. And keep the roof and walls from caving in.

Tunnels are made in different shapes. Round tunnels go through soft ground under rivers and bays.

Tunnels with straight walls and arched tops are better for holding up rock in a mountain.

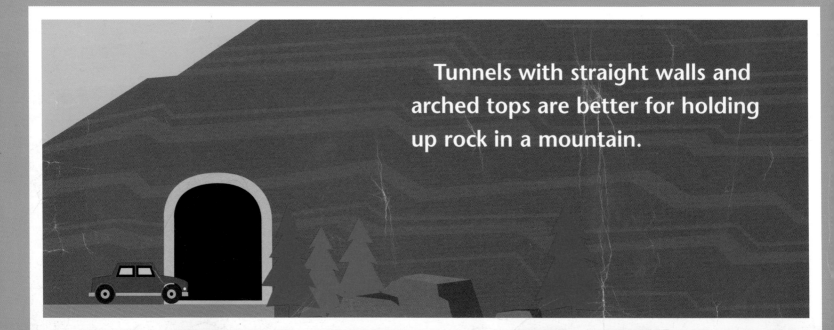

If you take a train from New York to Los Angeles you'll go through 65 mountain tunnels.

NEW YORK

CHICAGO

LOS ANGELES

N
W · E
S

A new kind of round tunnel will float across very deep waterways. It will be anchored to the bottom of the sea.

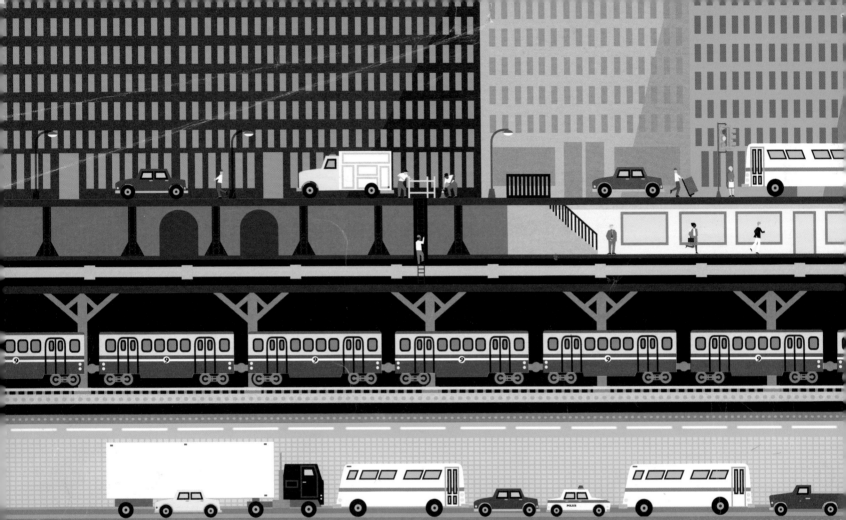

Now, tunnels run under cities carrying subways, cars, and people walking. They lead to shops and offices, factories and even swimming pools. Some people are planning whole cities underground. What would it be like to live there?